1800

THE
SLEEPING BEAUTY

BARRON'S
NEW YORK

First edition for the United States published 1989 by
Barron's Educational Series, Inc.

Copyright © in this edition
Century Hutchinson Ltd 1988

First published 1988 by
Hutchinson Children's Books
An imprint of Century Hutchinson Ltd
London, England.

Designed by ACE Limited

All inquiries should be addressed to:
Barron's Educational Series, Inc.
250 Wireless Boulevard
Hauppauge, New York 11788

Library of Congress Catalog Card No.   88–19348

International Standard Book No. 0-8120-5965-4

Library of Congress Cataloging-in-Publication Data

Morin, Edmund.
    The Sleeping Beauty/Edmund Morin; adapted by Josephine Poole. – 1st ed.
    p.   cm. — (Picture classics)
    Summary: Doomed to sleep for 100 years by a wicked fairy, a
beautiful princess finally awakens with the kiss of a prince.
    ISBN 0–8120–5965–4
    [1. Fairy tales.   2. Folklore – Germany.]   I. Poole, Josephine.
II. Title.   III. Series.
PZ8.M825S1   1989
398.2'1'0943 — dc 19
[E]   88–19348
                                                              CIP
                                                               AC

PRINTED IN ITALY

THE
SLEEPING BEAUTY

ILLUSTRATED BY
EDMUND MORIN
RETOLD BY JOSEPHINE POOLE

SERIES EDITOR · ELIZABETH RUDD

BARRON'S
NEW YORK

Long ago there lived a king and queen who loved one another dearly but had no children. Oh, how they longed for them! And, at last, after many years, their prayers were answered – the queen gave birth to a daughter.

The joyful king arranged a splendid christening.

In those days, most royal children had a fairy godmother. But this little princess had seven, because seven fairies lived in her father's kingdom. After the christening, they drew near to lay their magical hands upon the baby. The first gave her beauty, and the second, wisdom; the third said she would be graceful in all she did; the fourth, that she would dance as lightly as a leaf upon a tree; the fifth, that she would sing like a nightingale; the sixth, that she would play all kinds of musical instruments perfectly. The seventh godmother was about to speak when there was a bang and a puff of smoke! In darted a wicked old fairy! She was furious because the king, not knowing of her existence, had neglected to invite her to the christening. Everyone trembled as she announced, in a voice brimming with spite, "The child shall pierce her finger with a spindle, and die of the wound!"

Then the king drew his sword, though he knew it was useless, while the poor Queen began to weep. But the seventh godmother stepped forward. "I cannot undo this terrible wish," she said. "I can only promise that your daughter will not die when she pricks her finger. She will fall asleep, and sleep for a hundred years, until a king's son comes to awaken her."

The next day the king sent out his trumpeter, and proclamations were read and bonfires lit throughout the land, so that in a short time every spindle in the kingdom was burned to ashes.

As the years passed, the princess grew more and more beautiful, graceful and intelligent – just as her six godmothers had promised – until she was the most enchanting maiden in the world. For this reason, everyone called her Beauty.

When she was sixteen, Beauty accompanied her parents on a visit to a distant castle, and during a reception in the great hall, she went off by herself to explore. She found a twisting staircase, so dark and cramped it seemed only mice and spiders could live there. Up and up it led, and up she climbed, until she came to a door. She opened it, and found herself in a strange old-fashioned room, at the top of a tower.

There sat an old, old woman, dressed all in black, with a white muslin cap on her head, and glasses on her nose. She was spinning thread from a bundle of flax.

"What are you doing?" asked Beauty. "Please let me try!" And she reached for the spindle. But no sooner did she touch it than the sharp point ran into her hand. She gave a cry and fell fainting to the ground.

The king and queen heard the old woman's shrieks for help, and, rushing upstairs with beating hearts, they discovered poor Beauty lying senseless on the floor. They were filled with terrible grief. But the king remembered the good fairy's promise – that she would not die, but must sleep for a hundred years, and that a prince would come to wake her. So he lifted her in his arms and carried her to the finest room in the castle. There he laid her upon a bed which was all embroidered with gold and silver. Her little dog jumped up, curled at her feet, and would not be separated from her.

How quickly the sad news spread, and what weeping and sobbing filled the kingdom! For everyone loved Princess Beauty, from the pompous old Judge, with his heavy seals and books of wisdom, to the little boys who scared the crows away from the corn.

Now the sky turned black, there was a prolonged rumble of thunder, and the anxious king and queen hurried on to the top of the castle in case there was another disaster. Not at all: it was the seventh godmother, arriving in a chariot drawn by a perfectly matched pair of dragons, to comfort the grief-stricken parents.

"Oh, what will become of my dear child, when she awakes after a hundred years?" sobbed the Queen. "She will find herself among strangers, or worse, in a tumbledown castle full of dust and cobwebs!"

"I have the answer to that," said the fairy. And this was her kindly thought: to touch every living creature in the castle with her wand, so that each fell asleep, and slept until Beauty awoke.

But she would not touch the king and queen. So they kissed their beloved daughter for the last time, and then, returning sorrowfully to the palace, made a declaration, announcing that the castle was enchanted, and that nobody was to enter it under penalty of death. As it happened, within a short time there grew up around it such a forest of trees, bushes and brambles, all tangled up together, that neither man nor beast could get through.

All that could be seen were the tops of the towers. Inside, the lords and the ladies slept. The butler, the cooks and maids, the footmen, the grooms and horses, the dogs, the cats and chickens all slept – even the yellow canary that belonged to the princess snored with a whistle on his perch.